How Zebras Got Their Stripes

A tale from Africa

Retold by Lesley Sims

Illustrated by Laure Fournier

Reading consultant: Alison Kelly
Roehampton University

This story is about

a greedy
baboon,

a pond,

a giraffe,

an elephant

and the
very first
zebra.

Long ago, there was a greedy baboon.

He lived by a pond.

He wanted the pond all to himself.

Everyone was thirsty.

Baboon didn't care.

7

Giraffe crept to
the pond.

Baboon **roared**.
He waved his arms and
jumped up and down.

Giraffe fled.

Elephant went to
the pond.

Baboon **roared**. He jumped up and down and waved his arms.

Elephant fled.

Zebra walked up.

Baboon **roared.**
Zebra stamped his hoof.

"It's not your pond," he said. "You must share it."

"No!" said Baboon.
"Go away."

Baboon got lots of sticks.

He piled them by
the pond.

Zebra wasn't scared.

He ran at Baboon.

He kicked out his legs.

Baboon flew into the air.

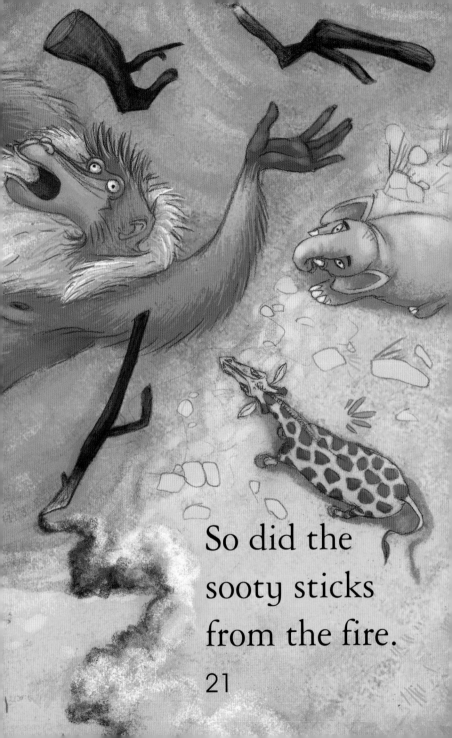

So did the
sooty sticks
from the fire.

The sticks landed
on Zebra.

Baboon landed on his bottom.

Ever since then, zebras have had black stripes.

And baboons have had
red bottoms.

Puzzles

Puzzle 1
Put the pictures in order.

A   B   C

D   E   F

Puzzle 2

A

B

C

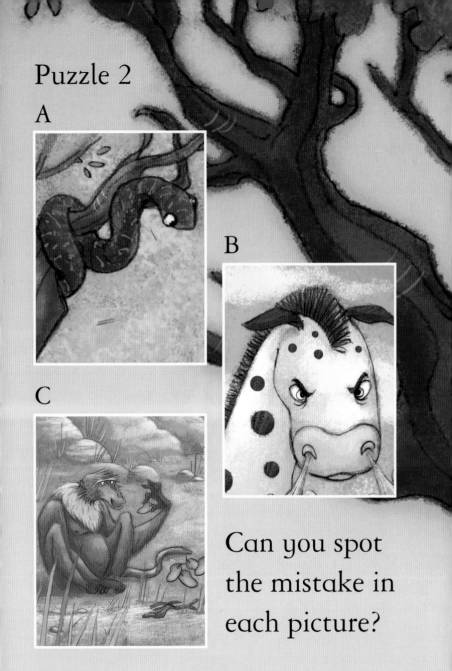

Can you spot the mistake in each picture?

Puzzle 3
Choose the best sentence.

Puzzle 4
Can you find these things in
the picture?

Elephant   Giraffe   pond
Zebra   Baboon   tail
bananas   trunk

Answers to puzzles

Puzzle 1

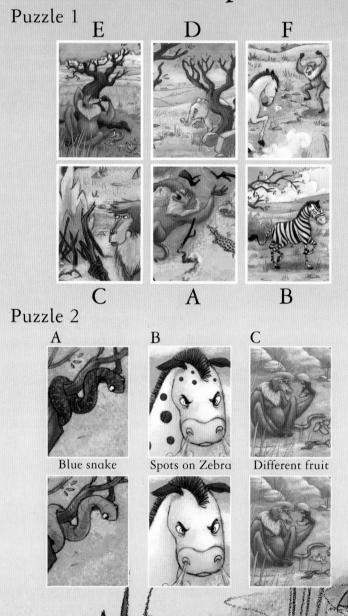

E   D   F

C   A   B

Puzzle 2

A — Blue snake

B — Spots on Zebra

C — Different fruit

Puzzle 3

A

B

Puzzle 4

About the story

This story is based on an old folk
tale from Namibia in Africa.

Designed by Nancy Leschnikoff
Additional design by Emily Bornoff
Series designer: Russell Punter

First published in 2009 by Usborne Publishing Ltd., Usborne House,
83-85 Saffron Hill, London EC1N 8RT, England. www.usborne.com
Copyright © 2009 Usborne Publishing Ltd.

USBORNE FIRST READING
Level Three

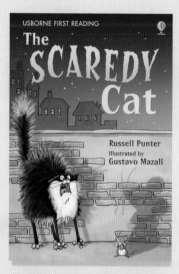

USBORNE FIRST READING

The **SCAREDY Cat**

Russell Punter
Illustrated by
Gustavo Mazali

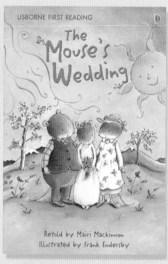

USBORNE FIRST READING

The Mouse's Wedding

Retold by Mairi Mackinnon
Illustrated by Frank Endersby

USBORNE FIRST READING

The **Magic Pear Tree**

Retold by
Rosie Dickins
Illustrated by
Matt Ward

USBORNE FIRST READING

The **Old Woman** who swallowed a Fly

Illustrated by
Sarah Horne